邱錫川吾兄惠存

陳亨詼 敬贈

2001年 4月 21日

游於藝

Searching joy & enjoyment in the art

胡朝景畫集

Hu Chao-Ching : A Collection of Works

目　錄

CONTENTS

朝景是三年前我在研究所指導的學生之一。在學期間，謙遜內斂，勤奮用功；其作品無論是意念的傳達或畫面的處理，都有傑出的表現，尤以畢業創作展「畫中畫系列」（民國八十七年五月）最令人感動，迄今餘韻猶存。可貴的是，朝景並不以此自滿，近幾年來，除了教學工作外，在創作研究上亦能孜孜不倦，未曾間斷。

有別於以往大場景的作品，朝景改以較精緻的畫面經營引人共鳴，同樣具有張力與厚度，而且更加溫馨、感人。此次個展中的自畫像系列作品，均以特殊的視點來呈現，詮釋畫者的心緒與環境、往事、記憶…之間的關係，雖不見主角的五官神韻，卻能隱約聽到他想透過畫筆傳達的訊息。其他作品，亦見跳脫了陳舊的構圖模式，以一種新的相貌呈現在觀眾面前，一景一物都充滿生命，恍若能在畫面中彼此對話，又同時和作品前駐足的觀眾相互心靈感通。

對一位創作者而言，天賦與勤奮同樣重要。天賦與生俱來，若空有天賦而不用功，則一切將成枉然；勤奮可以練就技巧，但徒有熟練的技巧也只能說是一名藝匠。唯有發揮天賦與勤奮不懈才能造就一流的藝術作品。

朝景有豐沛的才華，也有勤勉的特質，加上他對藝術的執著，相信他今後一定會繼續推出感人的作品。

於其個展之際，特綴短文祝福，並以為序。

陳景容

I met Chao-Ching three years ago when he was one of my students at the research institute. He is a humble and diligent young man. His works stand out in terms of the expression of ideas or the looks of painting. What worth mentioning is a series of works for his graduation in May of 1998. That was touching and I could still feel it now. But, he was not conceited with such accomplishments. Apart from his teaching work, he hammers on in his creation and study.

Departing from his usual big-scene works, his paintings are now turning out delicate but are still full of tensility and powerfulness, and even warmer and more touching. At this specific exhibition, the series of self-portrait are delivered and presented through a very special sight spot, interpreting the artist's inner side where his moods intertwine with his living environment, his past and memories. You don't see clearly the looks of the portrait, but you can hear indistinctly the message the artist tries to convey by way of his paintbrush.

On his other works, new looks are presented by jumping out of his usual way of sketching. Everything shown on his paintings is full of life and dialogues seem to be going on within. The viewers standing in front of the art piece are drawn to echo the same.

For an artist, God-given gift and diligence are both equally important. Without hard-working, the gift could be wasted. Diligence might help perfect your skills, but without gift you could end up an artisan. There is only one way to make a first-class artwork happen, that is, by fully exercising gift and diligence you have.

Chao-Ching is gifted and diligent. With his commitment to arts, I believe he will continuously create new works that move your heart.

By taking the occasion when his individual exhibition takes place, I wish him the best

Chen, Ching-Jung

有一天，愛因斯坦參加朋友的聚會，閒談間有名少女受到大師風采所吸引，好奇的詢問道：

「請問您是做什麼的？」

「我是研究物理學的。」愛因斯坦謙虛的回答。

「真的啊！那您今年幾歲了呢？」小女生問。

「老囉！都快八十啦！」大師笑著說。

「八十歲？怎麼您老人家這麼大的歲數，還在讀物理呢？人家我去年就PASS了。」

如果物理學只是一本書，也許很快可以讀完畢，不過，物理學畢竟是門學問，那就不一樣了。學無止境，活到老學到老，任何學問真要研究起來，唯有終身學習才是研究學問的態度。

朝景自幼喜歡塗鴉，至師專時期開始接受科班的訓練；就讀台北市立師範學院及師大美術研究所期間，一直努力不懈的增長自己在美術方面的知能。現在雖然已經獻身於美術教育工作，仍然在作育英才之餘，不忘隨時惕勵自己多畫多思考，堅持在美術創作的領域中持之以恆的努力，將繪畫與創作當作是終身的職志。

朝景的繪畫技巧嫻熟，風格平實自然，喜歡在生活中紀錄感情與感性；猶如魏斯的「老房舍」、梵谷的「破軍靴」，作品之中在在都流露出真誠自然的情感。

以朝景沉穩內斂的個性及豐富的才情，加上孜孜不倦的努力，未來必不可限量。這次他集結了兩年內的近作，開畫展以饗觀眾。

謹以一篇短文為序，特此致意，祝賀成功。

李 錫 津

One day, Einstein went to a friend's party. During an idle conversation, a young lady, attracted by the master's mien asked out of curiosity: "What's your profession?"

"I do physics research." Einstein humbly replied.

"Really! How old are you?" the young lady asked.

"I'm old! Almost 80!" the master laughingly replied.

"80? How could you still be studying physics at your age? I passed it last year."

If physics is a book, then perhaps one could finish reading it in no time, but physics is a field of science, and that's what makes the difference. One could never stop learning, one could learn, as one grows old. The true acquisition of knowledge is made possible through a lifetime of learning.

Chao-Ching loved to doodle since childhood, but he began formal training at the Normal College. As a student at the Taipei City Normal College and the National Taiwan Normal University graduate school, he diligently studied for the enhancement of his artistic skills. Now, following a career as an art educator, he would still push himself to draw and think whenever he had a break from teaching. He made a resolve to follow a lifelong career to concentrate his efforts in the field of creative art, and make painting and creativity his lifelong vocation.

As the painting skills matured, the style would naturally flow. he loved to record the emotions and sentiments of life; such as Andrew Wyeth's "The Old House", Van Gogh's "The Broken Boots"; one could feel the honest and natural emotions pour out of those paintings.

Mature and deep personality, rich talent and add then indefatigable diligence, and the future will know no bounds. This exhibit shall display two years of artistic work. I hope that this brief conveyed my admiration for his talent. Wishing you all the success in your show.

Lee, Hsi-Chin

序 —— 胡朝景

Foreword

「志於道、據於德、依於仁、游於藝」，……能如魚得水般的悠游在藝術領域中，是幸福，更是努力的目標。

一直希望能藉著畫筆來詮釋眼中的世界，在創作的過程中，我不斷嘗試使用各種方式，來表達自己心中的想法。「寫實」，在我的作品中是主要的表現方式，以此為主軸來發展不同的創作方向。譬如：虛實收放的強調與掌握、視點上的變化以及合理性的突破。

對一個以寫實為主要表現方式的創作者而言，很容易拘泥於繁複的細節或描繪的技巧，而使作品流於呆板、俗氣，令「寫實」變成「寫死」，事半功倍，甚為可惜。俄國文學家托爾斯泰說的好：「畫家是個能畫能塗的人」所謂「能畫」，指的是描繪的能力，是畫家形而下的功夫；所謂「能塗」，則指技巧的昇華，是畫家形而上的精神內涵。二者看似對立，實則相輔相乘。然而，如何將虛實收放在畫面上掌握得恰到好處，仍是個人不斷研究的課題。

除了虛實收放之外，我亦改變以往習慣的表達方式，嘗試以誇張的視點及突破畫面元素的合理性來營造特殊的氣氛。例如：「自畫像系列」中，我採取由正上方向下看的視點來作畫，感覺就像自己的靈魂脫離枷鎖般的軀殼來自我檢視一般。同樣的方式運用在許多靜物作品上，往往可以在平凡無奇的對象中創造令人驚異的效果。

我的作品構成元素簡單、自然。從日常生活中取材，以靜物、風景為主，並加上個人主觀情感的表達。這類題材，早已被認為陳腔濫調，了無新意，很難再有超越性的表現。然而，我仍努力在陳舊中發覺新意，於平凡中表現美感。作品中沒有深奧的人生哲理，或直指人性的病態現象，也不以一味的求新求變來譁眾取寵，或用充滿震撼力、侵略性的表現方式來給人當頭棒喝。我專注於畫面的溫馨感人，觸動人心。不斷在平凡無奇的題材中尋找發揮表現的廣度和深度，創造動人心弦的力量，使藝術生命得以久遠。

最後，謹以本書獻給曾指導、協助過我的師長及親友們。同時也要感謝陳教授景容和李局長錫津的賜序，使本書增色不少。

"Searching Joy and Enjoyment in The Art."It has been my constant wish and happiness to immerse myself in art. It is also a goal that I have been after.

By using the paintbrush, I always wish to interpret what I see. During the course of my creation, by using different ways I try the best I can to express my ideas. "Realism" is the core of my works. With it, my different approaches for creations are developed. For example, the emphasis and grasp of falsehood and reality, the changes on sight spots and the departure from reasonableness.

For an artist of realism, he tends to be bound to details or skills of painting which would eventually kill his artworks. Tolstoy, the Russian litterateur, made a good remark on this respect. He said that a painter is one who can paint and scribble. Actually he meant the ability to paint is the painting skill which is concrete, and the ability to scribble is the sublimation of his skill which is metaphysical and from which the essence of his works comes into being. It seems that both stand against each other. Actually, they co-exist nicely. However, it has been my constant focus to finely grasp the mystery that lies in between falsehood and reality on my works.

Besides, by using exaggerated sight spot and departing from reasonableness of screen element I have changed my customary way of expression to create a special atmosphere. For instance, the series of "self-portrait " are painted by looking down from above. Such a sight spot puts me in a position where I feel my soul is unleashed from my body enabling me to take a look at myself. By applying the same way to numerous still lives, I find that an amazing effect can be created and achieved on even an ordinary object.

My works are simple and natural. Daily life is the theme of my artworks which mainly are in the form of scenery and still life. My personal subjective feelings add another touch to them. Materials of the sort have been long regarded as commonplace, nothing new and rigid. Still, I make efforts to discover life and exhibit the beauty from the ordinary. You don't find from my works the profound philosophy of life or any criticism about morbid human natures. I don't try to be fanciful to stand out of the crowd or use riveting and aggressive approaches to deal a blow upon someone. My works are there to touch your heart and give you warmth for life. I am committed to creating arts out of the ordinary.

This book is dedicated to those who have ever supported me in my works. My appreciation also extends to Professor Chen, Ching-Jung and Lee, Hsi-Chin, the Director of Bureau of Education. Their prefaces help add a finishing touch to the book.

Hu Chao-Ching

「在平凡無奇的題材中尋找發揮表現的廣度和深度，創造動人心弦的力量，使藝術生命得以久遠。」

My works are there to touch your heart and give you warmth for life. I am committed to creating arts out of the ordinary.

簡 歷

1970	生於台灣省屏東縣
1991	省立新竹師範專科學校美勞科畢業
1997	台北市立師範學院美勞教育學系學士
1998	國立台灣師範大學美術研究所藝術學碩士
1990	新竹師專院慶美展國畫優選
1991	新竹師專美勞科畢業美展油畫優選
1991	假竹師畫廊舉辦第一次個展（生活日記）
1995	全省公教美展油畫優選
1995	全省公教美展水彩優選
1997	市立台北師範學院美勞教育學系第一名畢業
1997	全省公教美展專業組水彩第二名
1997	榮獲陳銀輝教授獎學金優秀獎
1998	榮獲第十屆奇美藝術人才培訓獎
1998	假師大畫廊舉辦第二次個展（畫中畫）
1999	榮獲第十一屆奇美藝術人才培訓獎
1999	跨世紀油畫研究協會會員
2000	應邀參加 2000 年台北縣美術家大展
2001	應邀參加 2001 年台北縣美術家大展
2001	假立大藝術中心舉辦第三次個展（游於藝）

Profile

1970	Born in Pingtung, Taiwan
1991	Graduated from Dept. of Arts & Crafts, Taiwan Provincial Hsin-Chu Junior Teachers College
1997	Bachelors in arts & crafts education, Taipei Municipal Teachers College
1998	Masters in Art, Graduate School of Art, National Taiwan Normal University
1990	Special Award in Chinese Painting, Hsin-Chu Junior Teachers College Art Exhibit
1991	Special Award in Oil Painting, Hsin-Chu Junior Teachers College Graduation Exhibit
1991	First one-man show at the Hsin-Chu Junior Teachers College Art Gallery (Life Diary)
1995	Special Award in oil painting, Provincial Public Servants & Teachers Art Exhibit
1995	Special Award in watercolor painting, Provincial Public Servants & Teachers Art Exhibit
1997	Summa cum laude, Taipei City Normal College Industrial Arts Education
1997	Second Place, Watercolor Category, Provincial Education Art Exhibit
1997	Prof. Chen In-hui Scholarship Excellence Award
1998	10th Chi-Mei Art Talent Training Award
1998	Second one-man show at the NTNU Art Gallery (Painting within a Painting)
1999	11th Chi-Mei Art Talent Training Award
1999	Member, Cross Century Oil Painting Research Association
2000	Invited exhibitor, 2000 Taipei County Artists' Exhibit
2001	Invited exhibitor, 2001 Taipei County Artists' Exhibit
2001	Third one-man show at the Li-Ta Art Center (Searching Joy and Enjoyment in The Art)

游於藝
油畫
2000
91 × 72.5 cm

Searching Joy and Enjoyment in The Art
Oil on Canvas
2000
91 × 72.5 cm

事事煩心
油畫
2000
116.5 × 80 cm

Everything is vexatious
Oil on Canvas
2000
116.5 × 80 cm

烙痕

油畫

2000

130 × 89 cm

———————————

Brand

Oil on Canvas

2000

130 × 89 cm

憶
水彩
2000
109 × 78.5 cm

Memory
Watercolor
2000
109 × 78.5 cm

油畫
2000
45.5 × 38 cm

Oil on Canvas
2000
45.5 × 38 cm

油畫

2000

65 × 50 cm

Oil on Canvas

2000

65 × 50 cm

油畫

2000

53 × 41 cm

Oil on Canvas

2000

53 × 41 cm

油畫
2000
45.5 × 33 cm

Oil on Canvas
2000
45.5 × 33 cm

油畫
2000
45.5 × 33 cm
_____
Oil on Canvas
2000
45.5 × 33 cm

油畫

2000

41 × 27 cm

_____

Oil on Canvas

2000

41 × 27 cm

油畫
2000
41 × 27 cm

Oil on Canvas
2000
41 × 27 cm

油畫
2001
33 × 21 cm
————————————————
Oil on Canvas
2001
33 × 21 cm

油畫
2000
53 × 45.5 cm
_____

Oil on Canvas
2000
53 × 45.5 cm

油畫

2000

25.5 × 17.5 cm

Oil on Canvas

2000

25.5 × 17.5 cm

油畫

2001

53 × 33.5 cm

_____

Oil on Canvas

2001

53 × 33.5 cm

油畫

1999

45.5 × 38 cm

Oil on Canvas

1999

45.5 × 38 cm

油畫
2000
45.5 × 33 cm

Oil on Canvas
2000
45.5 × 33 cm

油畫
2001
41 × 27 cm

Oil on Canvas
2001
41 × 27 cm

油畫

2001

33 × 24 cm

Oil on Canvas

2001

33 × 24 cm

油畫
2001
33 × 24 cm

Oil on Canvas
2001
33 × 24 cm

油畫
2001
41 × 24 cm

Oil on Canvas
2001
41 × 24 cm

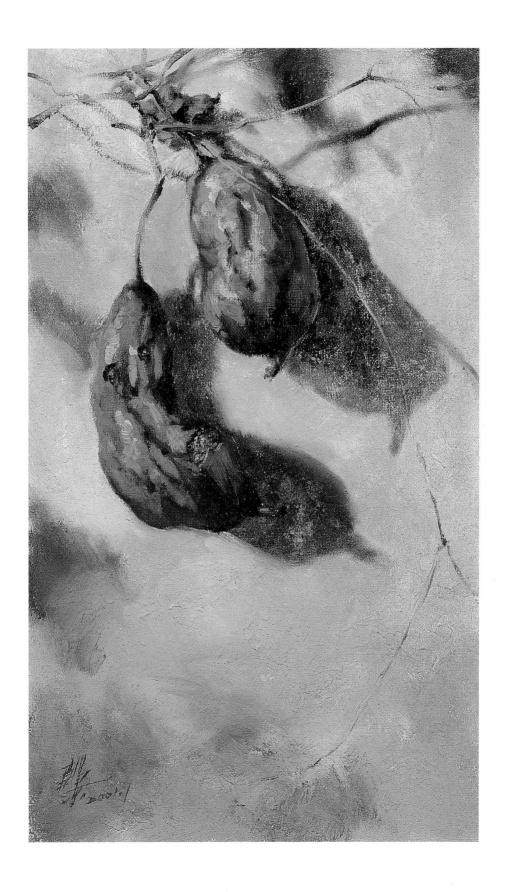

油畫
2001
33 × 21 cm

Oil on Canvas
2001
33 × 21 cm

油畫
2000
41 × 31.5 cm

Oil on Canvas
2000
41 × 31.5 cm

油畫
2001
25.5 × 17.5 cm
_____

Oil on Canvas
2001
25.5 × 17.5 cm

油畫
2001
25.5 × 17.5 cm

Oil on Canvas
2001
25.5 × 17.5 cm

水彩
2000
38 × 25 cm

Watercolor
2000
38 × 25 cm

水彩
2000
38 × 25 cm

———————————

Watercolor
2000
38 × 25 cm

水彩

2000

38 × 25 cm

———————————

Watercolor

2000

38 × 25 cm

游於藝

Searching joy & enjoyment in the art

作者：胡朝景　Hu Chao-Ching,Author

編輯：陳璵惇　Chen Yu-Dun,Editor

美術編輯：謝惠婷　Hsieh Hui-Ting,Art Editor

攝影：林裕翔　Top Man Photo Studio,Photography

出版者：胡朝景　Hu Chao-Ching,Publisher

台北郵政 9-566 號信箱　P.O.BOX 9-566,Taipei,Taiwan,R.O.C

E-mail:aveans@ms32.hinet.net　phone:0920266483

印刷：中華彩色印刷股份有限公司　China Color Printing Co.,Inc.

初版：2001 年 4 月　First Printing, April 2001

定價：400 元

作者為陳享敏之女婿

國家圖書館出版品預行編目資料

游於藝 ： 胡朝景畫集 ＝ Searching joy &
enjoyment in the art ： Hu Chao-Ching ： a
collection of works / 胡朝景作. — 初版.
— 臺北市 ： 胡朝景，2001[民90]
　　面 ；　　公分

ISBN 957-744-639-6(平裝)

1. 水彩畫 - 作品集 2. 油畫 - 作品集

947.5　　　　　　　　　　　90005096